Gift of Gab

D0067096

adapted by Cathy East Dubowski and Mark Dubowski

illustrated by the Thompson Bros.

SCHOLASTIC INC.

New York Toronto London Auckland Sydney
Mexico City New Delhi Hong Kong

Based on the TV series *The Wild Thornberrys*® created by Klasky Csupo, Inc.
as seen on *Nickelodeon*®

ISBN 0-439-25180-X

12 11 10 9 8 7 6 5 4 3 2 1   0 1 2 3 4 5/0

Printed in the U.S.A.

First Scholastic printing, April 2001

Prologue

Hi! I'm Eliza Thornberry. I'm twelve years old and part of your average family. I have a dad, a mom, and a teenage sister named Debbie. Well, there *is* Donnie—we found him in the jungle. And Darwin the chimpanzee? He found us.

Oh, yeah, about our house. It moves! It's a big safari-van called a Commvee. It's got a table and places to sleep and just about everything we need to camp anywhere. Would you believe it travels on land and water? We really need it because we travel all over the world. You see, my dad hosts this TV nature show, and my mom films it.

Okay, so maybe we're not that average. And between you and me, something amazing happened to me. It's really cool, but totally secret. And you know what? Life's never been the same. . . .

You want to know my secret? Well . . . promise not to tell anyone? Okay.

The secret is . . . I can talk to animals!

Here's the story of how it all began. . . .

Chapter 1

I'm the luckiest girl in the world!

That's what I thought as my family drove through the hot, dusty streets of a small village in western Nigeria.

Our first adventure—Africa! It was so different from home. But that's what I liked about it.

Mom and Dad had traveled here to make their very first nature film. It was so cool that Debbie and I got to come along.

But Debbie didn't think so. She wasn't even looking out the window. She was too busy polluting the air by painting her toenails with smelly red nail polish.

Suddenly Dad shouted, "Everyone have a look-see up that tree!" He was so excited, he totally forgot to watch his driving. The Commvee swerved back and forth. "It's a rare white-throated bee-eater! Somebody pinch me!"

Mom pinched him.

"Ouch!" Dad yelped, then added, "Thanks, pumpkin. And look," he gushed, "we've caught it actually eating a bee!"

Dad jerked the wheel. Debbie and I tumbled to the floor.

"Nigel, dear," Mom said, "maybe you'd enjoy the sights a little more if *I* were driving—and you *weren't*."

"Smashing idea, Marianne!" Dad said. He let go of the steering wheel and leaned out the window for a better look.

Unfortunately, he was still in the driver's seat.

Mom didn't freak out. She simply grabbed the wheel and steered our huge Commvee safely down the road.

I never did see that white-throated bee-eater. But that was okay. I had a feeling we'd see lots of unusual wildlife soon.

An hour or so later Mom stopped the Commvee in the middle of a clearing. It was the perfect place to make camp.

I looked out the window. Wow! This is so cool! Debbie was mad because she wanted to stay in a fancy hotel. But not me. Hotels are boring! With our Commvee we could sleep right out here in the middle of the wilderness. Who knew what we'd see?

I flew out of the Commvee. I was happy to be out in the fresh air—and away from

Debbie's stinky nail polish!

Mom and Dad quickly unpacked and set up their equipment—cameras, tripods, light meters, microphones—they were ready to film the beginning of their documentary.

"Hello," Dad said into the camera in his cheery British accent. (Dad is from England.) "Welcome to *Nigel Thornberry's Animal World.* . . ."

They would be busy for a while. That was okay with me. I was ready to explore the world!

When I was younger, Debbie used to play with me. But now she acts too cool to play. I mean, there we were, surrounded by the African jungle, full of untold secrets. And what did she do?

She sat down at the picnic table and dumped out all her makeup. Then she stared into a mirror at a pimple on the end of her nose that nobody else could even see.

Who cared? I set out to explore by myself.

The jungle around our clearing was thick and green. Suddenly I saw a cute, little gray chimpanzee standing a few yards away.

I didn't move. I didn't want to frighten it. "Hi, there," I said softly. I hoped I sounded friendly.

The chimpanzee shrieked and ducked back into the bushes.

Oh, if only I could talk to it. Really talk to it—in its own language. Then I could tell it not to be afraid. Hey! Maybe I can pretend to talk Chimpanzee! I leaned down and quietly chattered like a chimp.

The chimp stared back like it couldn't tell what to make of me. Then it scratched its head—and chattered back!

I felt like jumping up and down and cheering! But I didn't want to scare it. So I yanked on my pigtails and made more chimp-like sounds. I had no idea what I was saying. I hoped I hadn't accidentally said anything rude!

At last the chimp smiled. Slowly it came out of the bushes. Then it walked right up to me! Cool! No wonder my dad had picked studying nature for a career.

I saw that my parents were taking a break. So I led the chimp over to show my family. "Look what I found!"

My parents looked up in surprise.

"Fascinating!" Dad exclaimed. "They're not usually such social creatures."

Debbie's mirror flashed in the sunlight. The chimp wandered over toward the picnic table to see.

Debbie had her hair pulled back in a ponytail. She was putting some kind of weird goop on her face and neck.

The curious chimp looked over her shoulder into the mirror.

"Ewww!" Debbie screamed. She jumped up and threw a jar of face cream at it. "Get away from me, you chimpan-geek!"

The chimp cried and ran back into the bushes.

I was so mad! My parents love animals. And so do I. What was Debbie's problem?

"Debbie!" I exclaimed. "It didn't do anything! You don't treat a little animal like that!"

Debbie glared at me. "It seems to work with you!"

It was a mean thing to say. But I didn't care. I was too worried about the chimp. I turned and ran after it.

"Eliza! Wait!" Mom called after me.

But I had already disappeared into the jungle.

Chapter 2

"Hello!" I called out as I wandered deeper into the jungle. "Here, little chimp!" There were so many places here for an animal to hide. How could I ever find it?

I climbed over a log and kept walking. The trees and bushes seemed to move. I heard strange squawks and cheeps and growls. Were they friendly sounds? I wished I could understand what they meant.

Suddenly I heard a weird snorting noise—kind of like a pig eating peanut butter and jelly.

There, in the distance, lay a fat brown animal. It seemed to be rolling in the dirt.

As I crept closer, I heard a strange sound. A horrible sound. A sound like . . . pain!

I ran toward the animal. It was a large, hairy, warty warthog. I was surprised that it didn't run away.

And then I saw why.

The warthog's left hind leg was caught in the jaws of a big steel trap.

"Oh, you poor piggy!" I gasped. I can't stand to see animals in pain. I reached out to pet it. But it growled and lashed out at me with two big tusks that stuck out on either side of its mouth.

"I won't hurt you," I said in a soft voice. "I've got to get you out of there!"

I stood where I could reach its hind

leg—but where its scary teeth couldn't reach me! I tried to pull the trap open.

"Uhn!" I grunted as I struggled.

At first it wouldn't budge. The trap held the warthog's leg tight between its jagged teeth.

But I wouldn't give up. I *love* animals. Which means I also *hate* traps.

I tried again. My arms trembled as I pulled the steel jaws apart a few inches. But it was enough. The warthog pulled its leg free!

Then I let go.

Clang!

The force of the trap snapping shut sent me flying head over heels to the ground.

The fierce-looking warthog snorted and got to its feet. It trotted over and stared down at me.

I had freed the animal from the trap. But now *I* was trapped!

"Looks like your leg's okay now," I said with a shaky smile.

The beast took a step toward me. I gasped as it growled and shook its tail.

Then something amazing happened. It was one of the strangest things I have ever seen! A grass skirt appeared around the warthog's thick waist. A front hoof twisted, then morphed into—a human hand! And then it had two hands!

The warthog's groans were frightening, but I couldn't run. I couldn't stop watching.

Its back legs turned into—human legs! And then its big, hairy, warty face morphed into—a big, hairy, warty *human* face!

I closed my eyes and shook my head. Then I opened my eyes again. "No way!" I cried.

The fat, warty warthog had changed into . . . a fat, warty man!

Chapter 3

I rubbed my eyes. Was I seeing things?

I opened my eyes again. The man was still there.

He wore a feathered headdress and a grass skirt. His face looked a lot like the warthog's—same eyes, brown hair, plenty of warts, big belly. He even had a big bone through his nose.

The man seemed as surprised as I was. He wiggled his fat fingers. Then he threw his hands in the air and laughed. "I'm human again!" he shouted. "After all these years!" He shook my hand hard. "Oh, thank you, little girl!"

I stared at him. "But I saved a warthog!" I said. "How did you become a man?"

The man shrugged. "I guess you broke the spell."

I heard a huge rumbling sound. The man grabbed his belly. "Ooh. Got anything to eat? I'm starved."

I pulled an apple from my pocket. The man grabbed it and gobbled it down. Maybe he had changed into a man. But he still had the manners of a warthog!

Especially when he let out a big, deep "B-u-u-u-r-r-r-r-p!"

"Nice burp!" I said. Then I frowned. "What spell?"

The man began to snack on the leaves of a bush. "I used to be a high shaman in the Sarimba tribe," he explained. "We were a people who believed that animal and human spirits joined together. But the truth was, I couldn't stand animals!"

"That's terrible!" I said.

"That's what the Sarimbas said! Then I ate the really high shaman's prized sheep. He was so mad, he cast a spell that turned me into a warthog. But thanks to you, I turned back into a man!"

"Because I saved your life?" I asked.

"Exactly." The shaman leaned closer. "The spell could only be broken if a human really cared about me. But they figured, who would like a gross, smelly animal?"

"I would," I said.

"That's why I get to grant you a wish!" the shaman exclaimed.

"I get a wish?" I gasped. "Wow!" I couldn't believe it! The shaman waited patiently as I thought and thought.

Wouldn't you know it? My mind was a total blank! Then I heard a familiar sound. I looked into the trees. It was the little gray chimpanzee! "Hey!" I called.

The chimp chattered and hid among the leaves.

"I'm not going to hurt you!" I promised. But the chimp wouldn't come out. I sighed. "Oh, don't you understand?"

My heart sank. The little chimp was so cute. I *really* wanted to be friends with it. If only I could talk to it!

And then I smiled. I knew exactly what I wanted to wish for! "I want to be able to talk to animals!" I told the shaman.

"Well, that's a first," the shaman replied. "Let's see now, how does that one go . . ." Sparkles swirled around the shaman's right hand. And then—

Poof!

A stick with the head of a snake on one

end appeared in his hand. It was some kind of magic wand. The shaman raised his magic stick to the heavens and shouted, "OOBALA-BOOBALA BOOBALA-DOOBALA! Give this one a shadoo-bah!"

I held my breath. Nothing happened.

The shaman said, at last, scratching his head, "Hmm. Wrong one. How about—OOOBALABOOBALABOOBALA! She can talk to animals!"

This time *something* happened. A strange whirl of blue light spun from the mouth of the snake head on the end of the magic stick. It swirled around me. It nearly took my breath away. I watched as ancient symbols of animals danced in the swirling light. I could hear their squawks and growls and roars.

I was terrified. The shaman's magic was real! I felt so dizzy. With a gasp, I tumbled to the ground.

Chapter 4

I waited for the world to stop spinning. I caught my breath and blinked. I looked around. All signs of the magic were gone. The clearing was quiet and peaceful again.

"It's time for me to go!" the shaman said.

But what about my wish? I didn't feel any different. Had the magic worked? Did it come with instructions? "Hey, wait!" I cried.

But the shaman had disappeared.

Was this a joke? Was it a dream?

"Hey, that's my gerbil!" someone shouted.

"Gulp! Not anymore!" somebody replied.

I looked up into a nearby tree. Two meerkats were arguing. And I understood *every* word they said! The shaman's magic had worked! "Wow!" I exclaimed. "I understood that!"

I wandered farther into the jungle. "Hello," I called out. "Can anybody understand me?"

"There's a bug in your hair!" someone sang out in a cheerful British accent. "Can I have it?"

"Eeew!" I brushed at my hair. Then I realized: Somebody answered me! I looked up. It was the chimp I'd met that morning! "Wow!" I said. "You said that, didn't you?"

He sat up with a startled look on his face. "Wait a minute! *You're* speaking *Chimp!*"

"Yes!" I cried. "And I can't even speak French!"

The chimp dropped to the ground.

"Finally!" he exclaimed gleefully. "Someone *civilized* to talk to!"

"Finally!" I exclaimed just as gleefully. "Someone *uncivilized* to talk to!"

We grabbed each other's hands and laughed. I just knew we were going to be friends.

Chapter 5

The chimp showed me how to swing through the trees on vines. I told him all about my family. Hanging from both hands, I said, "By the way, I'm Eliza."

"My name is AH-ooh-ooh-ah," he screeched. "But my friends call me AH!"

"That's a little hard for me to say," I said. "Why don't I just call you . . ." I thought a moment. "Darwin?"

"I like that," the chimp said.

I smiled. "We have so much to talk about. Maybe you can stay with us!"

"Really?" Darwin exclaimed. "I thought you'd never ask!" Then he frowned. "But your parents might not want me to."

"Sure, they will," I insisted. "I'll talk them into it." I grabbed Darwin's hand and led him back to my family's camp. Darwin scampered over to our clothesline. He seemed spellbound by the freshly washed clothes.

"Hey," I said, "do you want to dress like us, too?"

Darwin nodded, so I pulled some clothes off the line. He smiled in delight as I slipped a blue-and-white-striped tank top over his head. Next I gave him a pair of blue shorts. I held up a mirror for him to see.

Darwin smiled. I could tell he was happy.

Then I heard my parents and sister coming out of the jungle. I hoped they were in a good mood. I wanted to ask if I could have a friend sleep over. Would they mind that my new friend was a chimp?

Mom and Dad were smiling. But Debbie stomped into camp as if she'd had the worst day of her life. She didn't even see Darwin at first. She dropped some equipment on the ground at his feet.

Then Debbie saw Darwin. "Ewwwwww!" she shrieked. Her eyes grew wide as she stared at Darwin's clothes. "Wait! I am going to barf! Is that revolting hair ball wearing my lucky top? Give it back!" she shouted. But when she saw him scratch, she turned away in disgust. "Eww! Just keep it!"

Darwin ran to my side. He was trembling. But when I took him by the hand, he seemed to calm down.

"Mom! Dad!" I said. "Guess what! I can talk to animals!"

My parents stared at me in astonishment.

I giggled. "I know it sounds crazy, but I really can."

At least, that was what I *tried* to say.

But something was wrong. Super wrong!

I suddenly realized why my parents were staring at me.

My thoughts didn't come out in human words. The sounds coming from my mouth were *animal* sounds!

"Eliza, is this a joke, honey?" my mother asked. "Why are you croaking like a frog?"

"I told you she was a loon," Debbie complained.

I shivered. I didn't know *what* was going on. I cleared my throat and tried again. "Mom, Dad, I can talk to animals. . . ."

This time, all my words sounded like gorilla!

Dad grinned in delight. He thought I was playing a game.

But this was no game. It was totally for real!

I tried to speak to them again. But all I could do was growl, chirp, cheep, hoot, and bark.

I turned to my new friend. "Oh, no, Darwin! Is this really happening? The shaman's spell—he got it all wrong!" I looked at my family—the people I loved more than anything in the world.

"I can talk to animals," I said. "But now I can't talk to *people*!"

Chapter 6

There was only one thing to do.

"Come on, Darwin," I cried. "We've got to find that shaman!"

Of course, to my family, it sounded like I said, "Oooh-ooh, eek-eek, squawk!"

I ran into the jungle with Darwin right behind me.

"Be back by nightfall, honey," my mom called after me. "Remember, we're leaving for Kenya!"

One thing about the jungle that's different from towns: There are no street signs. So if you want to find your way, you have to know how to read other signs. Like take a left at the tangled vine. Then look for three big rocks covered with slime.

I tried to remember which vines, rocks, bushes, and trees I'd seen on my way to the place where I met the shaman. But I kept getting mixed up.

At last Darwin and I came to a clearing in the jungle. Was this the spot? It was hard to be sure.

But one thing *was* for sure.

"He's not here," I said. "He's probably gone forever."

"Darwin, what am I going to do?" I exclaimed. I sat down on a big rock and propped my head in my hands. "I can't talk to my family anymore. What if I'm like this for the rest of my life?"

"Don't worry, Eliza," Darwin said. "You can still talk to *me*."

"I wanted to talk to animals so badly . . . ," I began. My throat clogged up. Tears began to trickle down my face.

Darwin sat down beside me. Tears welled up in his eyes, too. "Don't cry," he said with a sniffle. "You'll get me started and my nose will get all runny and my fur will get all matty and . . ." Darwin burst into tears and threw his arms around me.

Suddenly I heard a rumbling sound. The sound grew louder and louder. A huge shadow blocked out the setting sun.

I wiped my nose and looked up.

A tour bus drove by. It was old, red, and rickety. Many people sat inside.

Including a big, fat, warty-looking guy eating a chicken leg!

I jumped to my feet as the bus chugged

on by. "Darwin! It's the shaman guy! Come back! I need to talk to you!"

I tried to run after him, but it was no use. The bus was faster than I could ever run.

I watched as my one chance to get my wish fixed disappeared in a cloud of dust.

Chapter 7

Then I remembered my dad—the brilliant naturalist Nigel Thornberry. He was always wandering off to study some animal, bird, or bug. So he got lost a lot. Somehow though, he always managed to find his way back home. You know what he always says?

"Heads up! Carry on! Never say die. Come on, Eliza. You'll never get anywhere by sitting on your duff, my dear! A journey of a

thousand miles begins with a single step...."

Well, my red hair isn't the only thing I got from my father. "Come on, Darwin. I'm going to find us a shortcut through the jungle so we can cut off that bus!"

We walked and walked. But there was no sign of the road.

"Where are we, Eliza?" Darwin asked. He sounded scared.

"I don't know." I sighed. "I wish there was someone I could ask. But then, I'd probably just bark at them."

Then it hit me. "But I *can* talk to animals!" I exclaimed. "*They'll* help us!"

"Or eat us . . . ," Darwin said.

"No, Darwin," I promised. "They're going to love me." I pulled him along the path. "You'll see."

I spotted some bearded monkeys in a tree. Darwin and I climbed up to ask directions.

Their answer was to tickle Darwin till he shrieked.

"Will you please tell us how to get to the road?" I asked.

But they just started tickling me! We had to get away.

I grabbed hold of a thick vine. Together we swung to another tree. We sat there dangling our feet as we caught our breath.

Suddenly I froze as a huge, ugly bird landed right next to me. A vulture! It was bigger than I was. It stared at me with big, scary eyeballs. And it looked awfully hungry. . . .

"Uh, hello, nice vulture," I said politely.

I knew from Dad that vultures eat dead animals to help keep the Earth clean. This one looked at me like I was a cheeseburger. "Hmph! You're *way* too fresh for me to eat."

I gulped. "Um, sorry to bother you," I said politely. "But we got chased up this tree and we've got to find the—"

"Yeah, yeah, yeah," the vulture said rudely. Suddenly she pointed with her beak. "Hey! Look over there!"

Darwin and I looked.

The vulture spread her wings wide—and shoved the two of us right off the limb!

Darwin and I screamed. "Ahhhhhhh!"

Thud! Thud!

We landed in the dirt.

"What about now?" the vulture asked eagerly. "Are you starting to *fester* yet?"

I stood up. "No!" I replied. "And you didn't need to do that!"

The vulture just spread her wings and flew away.

"So, I'm seeing that all animals aren't so friendly," I said.

"Depends on who you talk to."

I looked up. That wasn't Darwin's voice! Who said that?

A white horse-like animal with two twisted horns on his head trotted into the clearing. "Some of us are charming," he added.

"Are you some kind of antelope?" I asked.

"They're my cousins! I'm a hartebeest," the animal said proudly. "Are you some kind of talking girl?"

"Yup. I'm an Eliza Thornberry," I said. "Do you know what a 'road' is?"

"Sure," the hartebeest said.

"Do you think you could take us there?" I asked.

The hartebeest shrugged. "I'm free most of the day." He bent his front leg and made an elegant bow. "Hop on!"

I climbed on and pulled Darwin up behind me. Then the hartebeest headed straight for the road.

Or so I thought.

We rode for half an hour. Then the hartebeest said, "Now, I know *what* a road is. I just don't know *where* it is."

My heart sank. I felt Darwin's arms hug me tight.

"So we're *all* lost," I said.

Chapter 8

I felt like giving up.

But then I jerked my head up at the sound of squawking. A flock of beautiful red birds stared down at us. Yes! I had an idea!

I quickly told the birds my problem. From high in the sky it was easy for them to spot the road we needed. Looking up, it was easy for us to follow them. Within minutes we had found the road.

"Thanks a lot, guys!" I called. "Have a

great time migrating to Cairo!"

The road wound up a rocky mountainside. Near the top, I spotted the bus parked by a fence. "That's it!" I cried.

Darwin and I jumped down from the hartebeest's back. "Thanks for the ride!" I exclaimed. The animal bowed, then he gracefully sprang off into the jungle.

At the top of the cliff we found lots of people waiting in line. But I didn't see the shaman anywhere.

"Five naira," said a man who sat near the entrance. When the people paid, he handed them a towel. "Enjoy the mud," he said. I figured the shaman must have gone inside.

Oops! The man dropped a towel. When he bent over to pick it up, Darwin and I dashed through the gate.

Inside we saw fat people. Skinny people. All soaking in mud baths. But nobody who looked like a warthog.

"B-u-u-u-u-u-r-r-r-p!"

I whirled around. "I'd know that burp anywhere!" I shouted.

Darwin and I ran toward the sound. We found the shaman up to his waist in mud. And he was still chewing on a chicken leg.

"Why did you disappear?" I demanded.

"To return to my old tribal hot springs," the shaman explained. "Ah! Nothing like a good mud wallow." He laughed.

"Look, mister, you goofed," I said. "I can't talk to people anymore!"

The shaman shrugged. "And that's a problem?"

"But I need to talk to my family!" I cried.

The shaman sighed. "Look, I can make you talk to animals *or* people—but not both. Who do you want to talk to?"

"This isn't fair!" I cried. "I made a new

friend named Darwin. We talk about *everything*. But"—I swallowed the lump in my throat—"I guess I can't go through life without talking to people. . . ."

Poof! Sparkles surrounded the shaman's fist. His magic stick appeared in his hand. "Okay, back to the way you were—"

"Wait!" I cried. "Wait—I just need a minute." I had to say good-bye to Darwin first. He was playing in his own pool of mud.

Slowly I walked over to him. He smiled at me. How could I tell him?

"Darwin," I said softly. "This has probably been the best day of my entire life! But . . . I need to talk to my mom. And my dad. And my sister—well, not so much to her. But you and me, Darwin—" I took a deep breath, then said the words I did not want to say—in any language: "We're not going to be able to understand each other anymore."

The look on his face nearly broke my

heart. Choking back tears, I said sadly, "There's nothing I can do. . . ." I forced my feet to carry me back to the shaman.

The shaman raised his fist in the air and shouted: "BAREEPLE-MEEPLE, SHE-CAN-TALK-TO-PEOPLE . . . Leeple."

He pointed his magic stick at me again. A bright light and sparkling colors blew around me. Only this time the sounds of animals screamed louder. This time the winds were even stronger. I felt as if I might be whisked away into the sky.

But the magic tornado simply tossed me into Darwin's pool of mud. "Agh!" I gasped.

"What's going on?" Darwin asked as he hovered around me like a mother hen. "What's he doing? What . . . "

Then his words changed into the wild chatter of a chimpanzee. A chatter I could no longer understand. I stared at him with tears in my eyes.

It was time to go home.

"Good-bye, mister," I said to the shaman.

I guess I should have felt lucky. After all, I had talked to animals—if only for a little while. That was more than other people ever had in a whole lifetime.

As I walked away I heard Darwin scolding the shaman in Chimpanzee. He jumped up and down like a little kid having a temper tantrum.

But the muddy ground was slippery. He lost his balance. I watched in horror as he fell and skidded through the mud on his stomach—toward the edge of the cliff!

"Oh, no! Darwin!" I cried.

I didn't stop to think of my own safety. I just ran—slipping and sliding in the mud—to save my friend.

But it was too late.

Darwin screamed—and disappeared over the edge of the cliff!

Chapter 9

I couldn't bear to look!

But then I heard chatter. Frightened *chimp* chatter! *Darwin?*

I dropped to my hands and knees. Carefully I crawled to the edge of the cliff. I took a deep breath, then made myself look.

Darwin clung to a branch. He was alive!

But below him raged a roaring river. If Darwin fell, I knew I'd never see him again.

"I'm coming to get you!" I cried. "Hang on!"

A branch stuck out at the edge of the cliff. Perfect! I grabbed on tight, then scooted on my stomach to the edge. Slowly, carefully, I lowered myself down toward Darwin.

At last I hung down straight. I could almost reach him—but not quite. I pointed my foot, stretching for an extra inch.

Darwin reached up one of his hands and grabbed one of mine with a tight grip. Yes!

But the branch was not strong enough to hold me *and* Darwin. It tore away from the cliff! I screamed as we fell toward the river.

But there was no splash! I opened my eyes. Somehow I had grabbed the branch that Darwin had dangled from.

Snap!

That's when the branch broke in two! I heard a piece splash in the water below.

My hands ached. How much longer could I hold on?

"Grab on, Eliza!" a deep voice suddenly boomed.

I looked up. The shaman! He leaned over the edge of the cliff and held out one of his hands.

I grabbed on tight, and the shaman yanked us up to the top.

Darwin and I lay gasping on the muddy ground. We were okay!

"Thank you!" I told the shaman. "Thank you! You saved us!"

The shaman looked embarrassed. But he smiled when he saw Darwin and me hugging like we'd just won a million dollars.

"Come on, Darwin," I said at last. "Let's go home."

As we walked away, Darwin chattered excitedly. But, of course, I couldn't understand a single word. That was the only sad part.

"Wait a minute," the shaman called out to us.

Darwin and I turned around.

The shaman's eyes had filled with tears. "I shouldn't be doing this, but—what the heck. There's a spell I heard about. Not an easy one. But if you're willing to give it a try, I am."

"Will I be able to talk to Darwin—and to people, too?" I asked.

"Yes! But if I get it wrong . . ." The shaman shrugged. "You might grow an extra head."

Ewww! That was a big risk. Was it worth it?

I looked at Darwin. Darwin looked at me and smiled. And I knew what I wanted to do. Good friends like Darwin aren't easy to find—in the city *or* in the jungle. When you find one, you should do all you can to hold on.

I turned back to the shaman. "Let's give it a try!"

"Okay," the shaman shouted. "Give her the deluxe spell!"

A dazzling orange light spun around me. The winds blew. Images of animals roared around my head.

Then the winds died. I fell to the ground on top of Darwin.

"Watch it!" Darwin complained.

I sat up. "I—I'm sorry. I—" Then my mouth hung open. I grabbed Darwin by the shoulders. "We're talking!"

"Yay!" he cried. We held hands and danced around.

"I can talk to *everything* now!" I shouted to the sky. I had never felt so happy in all my life!

The shaman climbed back into his mud bath and began to chomp on another chicken leg.

"I don't know how to thank you," I told him. "You've changed my life forever!"

He waved me over. "Just remember one thing," he warned me, his voice a whisper. "You must *never* tell a soul about these powers. If you do . . . the gift will disappear."

Never tell? Not even my mom and dad? How could he expect me to keep such a secret?

The shaman continued to stare at me.

I smiled. "I understand."

Then I ran to grab hold of Darwin's hand.

It was time to go home.

Chapter 10

It was dark by the time Darwin and I found our way back to camp. I saw my mom and dad in the moonlight. They were carrying a huge trunk toward the Commvee. They were packing up.

Oh, yeah. Tomorrow we were leaving for Kenya.

"Mom! Dad!" I cried. "Guess what?"

My parents gasped. I guess I did look kind of funny with mud smeared all over me.

But they didn't yell. They waited for me to explain where I had been.

I grinned. I was so full of wonderful feelings—stories of all the magical things that had happened to me in the jungle.

But I remembered the shaman's warning. *"You must never tell a soul . . ."*

No way was I going to risk losing this special gift!

So all I said was, "I have a new friend!" I reached out for Darwin's hand and pulled him into the circle of my family.

Darwin smiled a shy smile.

My dad seemed delighted. Mom shook her head in wonder. Debbie covered her face with her hands and groaned in horrified disgust.

But I didn't care. I had a wonderful new friend.

And now that I could talk to animals? I had a feeling the adventures had just begun.

Discovery Facts

Hartebeest: The hartebeest is an endangered species now that the African plains have become more developed. It is still a strong survivor. In fact, unlike many of its cousins, the hartebeest does not need drinking water as long as there are grasses and roots for it to graze on.

Meerkat: The meerkat looks like it is always wearing sunglasses because of the dark skin around its eyes which helps it to see in the bright light of the African plain. It lives in families of five to thirty members, known as "mobs."

Vulture: The vulture is a wild African scavenger— it eats the remains of dead animals. After a lion kill, the sky will fill with vultures, circling like planes over an airport, waiting their turn.

Warthog: Some say the warthog is Africa's ugliest animal, but not according to other warthogs! Like the elephant, the warthog is often hunted for its tusks. However, it is not nearly as protected by hunting laws as the elephant is.

About the Authors

Cathy East Dubowski and **Mark Dubowski** started writing and illustrating children's books while they lived in a small apartment in New York City. Now they work in two old barns on Morgan Creek near Chapel Hill, North Carolina. They live with their daughters, Lauren and Megan, and their two golden retrievers, Macdougal and Morgan. They also wrote the novelizations of both Rugrats feature films, *The Rugrats Movie* and *Rugrats in Paris,* and the Rugrats chapter books, *Chuckie's Big Wish* and *It Takes Two!*